R0055333934

FOUR
ON THE SHORE

by Edward Marshall
pictures by James Marshall

PUFFIN BOOKS

For Joe Bryans

PUFFIN BOOKS
Published by the Penguin Group
Penguin Putnam Books for Young Readers,
345 Hudson Street, New York, New York 10014, U.S.A.
Penguin Books Ltd, 80 Strand, London WC2R ORL, England
Penguin Books Australia Ltd, 250 Camberwell Road, Camberwell, Victoria 3124, Australia
Penguin Books Canada Ltd, 10 Alcorn Avenue, Toronto, Ontario, Canada M4V 3B2
Penguin Books (N.Z.) Ltd, 182-190 Wairau Road, Auckland 20, New Zealand

Penguin Books Ltd, Registered Offices: Harmondsworth, Middlesex, England

First published in the United States of America by Dial Books for Young Readers, 1985
Published in a Puffin Easy-to-Read edition, 1994

20

Text copyright © Edward Marshall, 1985
Illustrations copyright © James Marshall, 1985
All rights reserved
THE LIBRARY OF CONGRESS HAS CATALOGED THE DIAL EDITION AS FOLLOWS:
Marshall, Edward. Four on the Shore.
Summary: Hoping to scare away Willie, Spider's little brother, Lolly, Spider,
and Sam each tell a spooky story—but then Willie has a story of his own to tell.
1. Children's stories, American. [1. Ghosts—Fiction.] I. Marshall, James, ill.
II. Title.PZ7.M35655Fm 1985 [E] 84-15610

Puffin Easy-to-Read ISBN 0-14-037006-4

Puffin® and Easy-to-Read® are registered trademarks of Penguin Putnam Inc.

Printed in the United States of America

Reading Level 2.0

Lolly, Spider, and Sam
were doing their homework.
"Spider," said Lolly,
"your little brother is getting
on my nerves."

"Willie's just a kid," said Spider.

"We need some peace and quiet,"
said Sam.

"Let's go down by the lake,"
said Lolly.

"It's quiet there
and we can do lots of homework."

"That's a great idea!" said Spider.

"Let's meet at the lake
at six on the dot," said Sam.

"If our moms say yes."

At six on the dot

only Lolly and Sam

were at the lake.

"Maybe Spider's mom said no,"

said Lolly.

"Here he comes now," said Sam.

"Uh-oh," said Lolly.

"Look who is with him."

"Oh, no!" said Sam.

"He followed me," said Spider.

"That kid is trouble,"
said Lolly.
"He'll be good," said Spider.
"I promise."

"I'm hungry.

I'm thirsty.

I have to go to the bathroom,"
said Willie.

"See what I mean?" said Lolly.

9

Spider took his little brother
to the bathroom.

"We have to do something,"
said Lolly.
"And I have an idea."

10

"We're back," said Spider.

"Go throw rocks in the lake,"
Lolly told Willie.

And he did.

"Here is my idea," said Lolly.

"Let's tell stories," she said.

"The really scary kind.

The kind that make little kids

run home."

"It won't work," said Spider.

"You can't scare *him*."

"Let's all tell scary stories!"

said Lolly in a loud voice.

"Hot dog!" said Willie.

"I'll go first," said Lolly.

LOLLY'S
STORY

Once there was a mean old wolf.

"I sure am hungry,"

he told his wife.

"I'm sick," she said.

"Go out and eat something."

"I will," said the wolf.

In the forest the mean old wolf

saw a little boy

who looked *just* like Willie.

He had on roller skates.

"He might be too fast," said the wolf.

"I must be very, very clever."

"A wolf!" cried the little boy.

"*I* am a kitty cat," said the wolf.

"Come closer and I'll purr for you."

So the little boy came closer.

And the mean old wolf

ate him right up

roller skates and all.

And that was that.

"I'm hungry!" said Willie.

"See?" said Spider.

"I told you he wasn't scared."

"That story wouldn't scare a chicken,"
said Sam.

"Let *me* try!"

SAM'S
STORY

The little boy did not have skates.

He had a tricycle

with rockets.

And he got away.

Soon he came to a small house.

It was the kind of house

that witches live in.

But he did not know that.

"I see you," said a voice.

"But I don't see you,"

said the little boy.

"Step inside," said the voice.

"I don't know," said the little boy.

"Oh, come on," said the voice.

So he went in.

An old witch with green hair

was sitting up in bed.

"You are a witch!" said the boy.

"I cannot tell a lie,"

said the witch.

24

The little boy was really scared.

"Don't worry," said the witch.

"I only eat potatoes."

"Good," said the little kid.

"Will you stir that pot, dear?"

said the witch.

The little boy began

to stir the pot.

Then the mean old witch

cast a magic spell.

And she turned the little boy...

into a big, fat potato!

"Help! Help!" cried the potato.

The witch came closer and closer.

"She's going to eat me!"

cried the potato.

That night the mean old witch
had mashed potatoes for dinner.

And so did her two mean old cats.

Willie was no fun at all.

"I'm not scared of witches," he said.

"I know how to get him,"
said Spider.

SPIDER'S STORY

The magic spell did not work.

And the mean old witch

got so mad she just blew up.

The little boy got away.

Soon he came to a big old house.

It was the kind of house

that might be haunted!

"I think I'll go inside,"

said the little boy.

And he did.

But he made a big mistake.

He closed the door behind him.

And he locked it!

Then he heard a creepy noise.

It came from upstairs.

"I'll go see," he said.

And he went up the stairs.

"Ooooh," said a voice.

"It's coming from that closet,"
said the little boy.
He was very, very scared.

He opened the closet door and...

out jumped three ghosts!

And the little boy got so scared

he dropped dead!

So there.

"I used to be scared of ghosts," said Willie. "But not anymore."

"Okay, Mr. Smarty," said Lolly. "*You* tell a story!"

"Me?" said Willie.

"Let him try," said Spider.

WILLIE'S
STORY

The ghosts were very nice.

They gave the boy some apple pie.

"I must go now," he said.

"Don't go by the lake!"

said the ghosts.

"It's spooky down there."

But on the way home

the little boy took the wrong turn.

He could not read yet.

Soon he came to the lake.

The ghosts were wrong.

It didn't look so spooky.

"This is a nice place," he said.

Then the moon went behind a cloud.

And when it came out again

the little boy was...

a mean old vampire!

He had pointed ears,
long, sharp fangs,
and giant blue wings.

He had just eaten dinner.

"But I want dessert," he said.

"A big juicy kid will do."

Soon he saw what he wanted.

Closer and closer he flew.

He licked his fangs.

"Which one will be first?"
he said.

He was almost there.

"And then?" cried Sam and Spider.

"Do you really want to know?"

said Willie.

"Yes!" they cried.

"The vampire got closer and closer...."

Just then the moon went behind
a dark cloud.
And when it came out again,
Willie was not there.

"Where is he?" said Spider.
"Maybe he's a vampire!" said Sam.

They stayed very close together.

They did not move.

"Oooh," they said.

"Tra-la!" cried Willie.

Lolly, Sam, and Spider nearly died.

"Did you like it?" said Willie.

"It was okay," said Spider.

"But we weren't *really* scared."

"Do you want to hear a story
about a werewolf?" said Willie.

"No!" said the others.

And that was that.